Watty Piper's
TRUCKS

Illustrations by Ann L. Cummings

Copyright © 1978 by Platt & Munk, Publishers. All rights reserved under Interna-
tional and Pan-American Copyright Conventions. Printed in the United States of
America. Library of Congress Catalog Card Number: 77-87558. ISBN 0-448-46526-4
(Trade Edition); ISBN 0-448-13068-8 (Library Edition). Designed by Teresa Delgado,
A Good Thing, Inc.

Platt & Munk, Publishers/New York

A Division of Grosset & Dunlap

Everyone knows cars are used mainly to help people move from one place to another. Trucks, though, are used for much more. There are many kinds of trucks. Each one has a special purpose.

A STREET SWEEPER does nothing but clean. With big brushes on its underside, it washes and sweeps the streets and gutters.

A FIRE TRUCK puts out fires. All the equipment needed for fire fighting is built right into the truck. One piece is the ladder, which is used to reach upper storey windows. Another is the pump, which shoots water through the hose.

A TRACTOR-TRAILER has two parts. The tractor holds the engine and the cab, where the driver sits. It pulls the trailer, which carries the freight.

A LOGGING TRUCK has a powered crane that lifts and stacks logs. It also has knobby tires that help it over timber trails to the sawmill.

A MILK TRUCK is a kind of tanker. Tankers hold different liquids, from orange juice to gasoline. To keep the milk cool, a milk truck is lined with glass like a giant thermos bottle.

An AUTOMOBILE CARRIER makes sure that cars reach the showroom just as new and clean as when they left the factory.

A **CEMENT MIXER** has two motors. The first motor drives the truck. The second turns a big barrel of cement around and around, to keep the cement from hardening on the way to the work site.

A DUMP TRUCK and an **EARTH MOVER** work together. The earth mover digs dirt and loads it into the back of the dump truck. The dump truck carries the dirt away. To unload, the back of the dump truck tilts up, and everything pours out.

A TOW TRUCK, or wrecker, is called to the scene when a car breaks down or has an accident. It pulls the car to the repair shop.

A SANITATION TRUCK collects garbage from the streets. After the garbage is thrown into the back of the truck, a big scoop crushes it and stuffs it inside, making room for more.

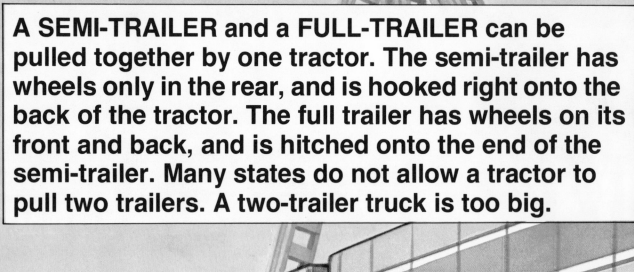

A SEMI-TRAILER and a FULL-TRAILER can be pulled together by one tractor. The semi-trailer has wheels only in the rear, and is hooked right onto the back of the tractor. The full trailer has wheels on its front and back, and is hitched onto the end of the semi-trailer. Many states do not allow a tractor to pull two trailers. A two-trailer truck is too big.

A MOVING VAN is wide and tall for holding bulky loads. It carries furniture and other belongings when a family moves. Everything must be packed and loaded carefully.

A STAKE TRUCK is used on a farm. Its wooden sides can be taken off in whichever way is easiest to load the truck—from the side, the back, or from all around.